This book belongs to:

_____

_____

_____

First published 2014 by Walker Books Ltd
87 Vauxhall Walk, London SE11 5HJ

This edition published 2015

2 4 6 8 10 9 7 5 3 1

© 2014 Lucy Cousins
Lucy Cousins font © 2014 Lucy Cousins

The author/illustrator has asserted her moral rights.

Illustrated in the style of Lucy Cousins by King Rollo Films Ltd

Maisy™. Maisy is a trademark of Walker Books Ltd, London.

Printed in China

British Library Cataloguing in Publication Data:
a catalogue record for this book is
available from the British Library.

ISBN 978-1-4063-5813-1

www.walker.co.uk

Maisy Goes to the Cinema

Lucy Cousins

WALKER BOOKS
AND SUBSIDIARIES
LONDON • BOSTON • SYDNEY • AUCKLAND

Today, Maisy and her friends
are going to the cinema.
"Oh, I am **SO** excited!" says Tallulah.
"Can we buy popcorn?" asks Charley.
"I LOVE popcorn!"

There are lots and lots of different films showing. What will they go and see?

Dusty Rider

HERO IN THE JUNGLE

SAM, THE HAPPY SHARK

A Royal Romance

Popcorn, a big drink, frozen yoghurt and ice cream— YUM!

Everyone likes adventure movies and Troy T. Tiger (a very BIG movie star) is starring in this one.

Wow! It's a BIG screen! Tallulah wants to sit in the middle and Cyril wants to sit next to Maisy.

Eddie and Charley want to sit at the very front!

The movie starts and the lights go down slowly...

Cyril doesn't like the dark cinema. "Don't worry, Cyril," says Maisy. "You can hold my hand."

"That's my *favourite* movie star!"
shouts Eddie when **Troy T. Tiger**
appears on screen.

Everybody in the cinema goes, "Shhhhhhhhhhh!" and "QUIET!"

Charley laughs so much that he spills all his popcorn on the floor!

It's nearly halfway through the film now and Tallulah needs the toilet.

"Me too," says Cyril.

"Me three!" says Eddie.

So they go as fast
as they can.

And wash
their hands
very quickly.

"Hurry! Hurry!"
says Eddie. They
don't want to
miss anything.

There's one very scary part
when Troy T. Tiger meets a
big, huge ... DINOSAUR!

"I can't watch!" says Cyril,
and he hides behind his hands.

Afterwards, Maisy and her *friends* all talk about their *favourite* part of the film.

"Let's go to see 'Hero in the Jungle' ... AGAIN!"

HERO IN THE JUNGLE